BROTHER GABRIEL AND

The Secret of Christmas

A Family Read-Aloud Book

Bob Hartman

ILLUSTRATED BY Matthew Archambault

Augsburg
MINNEAPOLIS

BROTHER GABRIEL AND THE SECRET OF CHRISTMAS
A Family Read-Aloud Book

Cover design by Marti Naughton
Book design by Marti Naughton and Michelle L. Norstad

Library of Congress Cataloging-in-Publication Data
Hartman, Bob, 1955–
    Brother Gabriel and the Secret of Christmas : a family read-aloud
book / Bob Hartman.
       p. cm.
    Includes bibliographical references (p.)
    Summary: Brother Gabriel uses his amazing flannelboard to explain
to Justin's Sunday school class the events of the Christmas story and the importance
of Jesus, even sending Justin and his friends back to witness the birth of the Christ
Child. Each chapter includes discussion questions and a prayer.
    ISBN 0-8066-3887-7
    1. Jesus Christ—Nativity Juvenile fiction. [1. Jesus Christ—Nativity Fiction.
2. Christmas Fiction. 3. Time travel Fiction. 4. Christian life Fiction.] I. Title.
  PZ7.H26725Br 1999
[Fic]—dc21   99-25818
                                                        CIP

Manufactured in Hong Kong. Printed by C & C Offset Printing Co., Ltd.
                                                      AF 9-3887

03   02   01   00   99   1   2   3   4   5   6   7   8   9   10

Contents

Introduction

❧

Seven or eight years ago, I wrote a series of picture books about Bible stories and Bible characters, each of which began with the same four words: "What was it like?"

One of the books told the Old Testament story of young Samuel. "What was it like in the middle of the night," I asked, "when God called the boy Samuel to be his prophet?"

"It was dream-like," I suggested. "It was scary. It was hard to sleep."

I asked the same question about Miriam, the young sister of baby Moses. "What was it like as she waited at the edge of the river and watched over her little brother?" I asked it about Adam, when he named the animals. And about a little boy in the New Testament named Levi who gave up his lunch of bread and fish so Jesus could feed a huge crowd.

My hope was that by asking the question—"What was it like?"—the children who read the books would be able to see themselves in those situations as well—to compare Samuel's fear with a time they were afraid, or Miriam's bravery with a time they had something hard to do. My hope was that, by crawling into those stories, the readers somehow would find the stories more "real"—and the God of those stories as well.

That is my hope for this book too. Through Brother Gabriel and his amazing flannelboard, I have tried to open a way "into" the Christmas story—a way for the children in the story and, hopefully, a way for you and your family too. It's a way that is consistent with the biblical material that forms the basis of the story. But it is also a way "between the lines" of the biblical accounts—a way of imagined details and characters and situations. And it is a way that asks questions about the Christmas story, the same questions I asked about Miriam and Samuel and Adam and Levi: "What was it like?"

The story itself will provide some of the answers. But to help you think about it more thoroughly, I have included a few discussion questions at the end of each chapter and a prayer to use, if you like. You could read a chapter each week, leading up to the holiday. Or you might find that you like the story so much you just can't wait that long!

However you decide to use this book, it is my prayer that as you and your family read the story and talk about it and pray over it, you will find the answer to the question, "What was it like?" And, in that answer, you may discover the answer to another, even more important question: "What is it like?" What is Christmas like for us today, and for people of all times? Both questions are really the same. One leads into the other.

And both questions will lead you, as they led the characters in the story, to discover the secret of Christmas.

Bob Hartman
Ben Avon, Pennsylvania

CHAPTER ONE

Brother Gabriel

"You can't trust Christmas!" said Brother Gabriel, grinning. And we just looked at each other, puzzled. Our regular teacher, Mrs. Anderson, had gone to visit her daughter for the holidays so, at the last minute, Brother Gabriel had volunteered to teach our Sunday school class.

He was a big man with a shining, black, bald head and a huge pair of hands. My uncle said he used to play football for the local college team. Somebody else said it was baseball. But it must have been years ago because his eyebrows and his mustache and the little bits of hair around his ears were almost pure white.

We were surprised to see Brother Gabriel turn up as our substitute teacher. He hadn't been coming to our church for very long. But Woodland Street Community Chapel was a pretty small congregation, perched on the side of a hill in one of the poorer parts of Pittsburgh. Help of any kind was hard to come by—that's what my mom was always saying—so I guess the leaders were happy to find anyone willing to teach the noisy collection of boys that made up our Junior Class. There was me—Justin; I was in fifth grade. And so was Darrell Jackson, who always came to church with his grandma. My cousin Bill was there too. He was in sixth grade. And Andy Chubb was in fourth.

"What do you mean?" asked Andrea Chalmers. (Oh, that's right: there was one girl too. She's a sixth grader—not enough for a class of her own, I guess.)

"Just what I said," Brother Gabriel answered with that same grin. "Christmas is a mystery, a surprise, a great secret! And it sneaks up on you when you least expect it."

"No it doesn't," argued Darrell Jackson. "It's just there—every December 25th. With presents and stockings . . ."

"And fruitcake!" added Andy Chubb.

"Cherries and nuts and little green things no one can identify," Brother Gabriel agreed. "Surprises. Just like I said." He reached behind his chair and pulled out a box wrapped with paper and ribbon, with a stick-on bow or two.

Suddenly, Sunday school was looking a lot more interesting.

"I bet it's candy," whispered Andrea.

"Or cookies!" wished my cousin Bill.

"Maybe it's a fruitcake!" added Andy Chubb.

"It's a surprise!" interrupted Brother Gabriel. "What have I been telling you? Now, somebody open it. Here . . ."

He handed the box to me.

I yanked off the bows, ripped the ribbons, and tore the paper underneath. But when I opened the box, there was no candy or cookies or even fruitcake to be found. There was just a musty smell; a tattered, brown piece of old flannel sheet; and a bunch of cutout felt figures.

"What kind of present is *that?*" somebody moaned.

"The best kind of all," Brother Gabriel answered. "A surprise!" Then he pulled out the sheet, unfolded it, and thumbtacked it to the wooden border of the blackboard.

"When I was a boy," he continued, "we had all our lessons on these flannelboards. The teacher would stick up the figures, one by one, then move them around to tell the story. David and Goliath. Noah and the Ark. And, of course, the first Christmas. It was amazing!"

Well, to be honest, I couldn't see anything amazing about the crude figures he hung on that old sheet. And neither could anyone else.

"What's that lump?" whispered Andrea.

"The blue one or the brown one?" snickered Darrell.

"I think it's a fruitcake," suggested Andy Chubb.

"It's a manger!" I said. "And Mary and Joseph and shepherds and an angel . . . I think."

"Good guess," said Brother Gabriel as he rubbed his hands together. "Now here's the best part," he said softly. "Look closely at Mary. Very close. You'll see what I mean."

We looked at each other first, not sure what to do or say. Nobody wanted to look stupid; and besides, what was there to see, anyway? Mary was just a blue triangle with a brown circle stuck on top.

And then Darrell tapped me on the shoulder. "Did you see that?" he whispered.

"See what?" I asked.

"Look! Look at Mary! Watch! She did it again. She *moved!*"

Darrell was right. The figure was moving. And it wasn't long before everyone could see. The room grew quiet and still, and I could tell that I wasn't the only one who had a creepy feeling.

"What did I tell you?" Brother Gabriel said with a smile.

"You can't trust Christmas. It sneaks up on you when you least expect it!"

We were all staring now. It was impossible to look away. Eyes and a nose and long black hair sprouted out of the circle that was Mary's head. The blue triangle became a robe, and two arms reached out from under the folds to lift what looked like a large, flat loaf of bread.

The manger was gone now, replaced by a rough wooden table. Joseph had left as well, along with the shepherds and their sheep. But the angel remained. And as we watched, he, too, filled out—from flannel to flesh and blood (or whatever it is that angels are made of!).

"Mary," the angel said—his words appearing in cartoon balloons above his head. "Mary, God has chosen you for something very special."

But Mary wasn't so sure. We could see the fear in her eyes and read her worried thoughts in the bubbles that popped up beside her face.

What does he mean? she wondered. *What does God want? And why would he choose a nobody like me?*

"Mary," the angel assured her. "There is nothing to be afraid of. God is very pleased with you. So pleased, in fact, that he has chosen you to give birth to a very special child."

The worried look on Mary's face now turned puzzled and confused. "But I don't understand," she said. "I'm not even married. How can I possibly have a baby?"

The angel smiled. "What is possible for us and what is possible for God are two very different things. He will send his Holy Spirit to cover you—like a warm summer shadow—and you will be the mother of God's own Son!" And then the angel added, very solemnly, "But only if you are willing."

Thoughts scrolled across Mary's bubble now, almost too quickly to read.

But how will I explain this? What will people say? And Joseph—my fiancé Joseph—how will he ever understand?

And yet . . . and yet . . . the mother of God's own Son! What an honor. What a responsibility. What a chance to show my God how much I want to serve him!

And so, before the words appeared, we knew what Mary's answer would be.

"I will do it," she agreed. "I will be whatever my God wants me to be."

And with that, the angel disappeared, and the speech and thought balloons along with him. Mary was left alone, the bread still in her hands and a wondering smile on her face. That's when the picture froze. And it was a minute or two before anyone spoke.

"How did you do that?" whispered Andrea.

"It's a video," shrugged my cousin Bill.

"Or a computer screen or one of those hologram things like on *Star Wars,*" suggested Darrell Jackson.

"It's a secret," Brother Gabriel said, grinning again. "One of those Christmas mysteries I've been telling you about. And if you keep watching, you'll see another."

We turned back to the flannelboard. Slowly, Mary began to change again. Her robe shrunk into an overcoat. Her long hair rolled back to her shoulders. And the bread in her hands turned into some kind of package.

"Hey! Hey!" shouted Andy Chubb. "I know who that is! That's that lady—the one who always sits at the back of the church."

"The one who smells kind of funny?" asked my cousin Bill.

"That's not very nice," said Andrea. "Does anybody know her name?"

I shook my head. "No. But, look! What's she doing now?"

"Watch. Watch and see," smiled Brother Gabriel.

A door appeared before the woman—a door like a thousand others in our part of the city, with a window on each side and a short stoop in front. And when the door at last cracked open, there was a much older woman peering out from behind.

The younger woman held the parcel out to the older one, and the smile that found its way between the two of them made both their faces beautiful.

"I wonder what's in the package?" I said out loud. And, just like she heard me, the old woman started to unwrap her gift.

"I don't believe it!" said Andrea.

"It can't be," muttered my cousin Bill.

"I think it is," sighed Darrell Jackson.

"It's a fruitcake!" chuckled Andy Chubb.

And so it was.

As we stared at the flannelboard, the figures turned back into felt shapes again. Then Brother Gabriel leaned over and whispered: "Nobodies. The nobodies known only to God. Like the young girl from Nazareth engaged to Joseph the carpenter. Or this woman whose name you don't even know. Humble servants. Selfless givers. Ministers of quiet kindness. Their gifts are the ones that bring joy to the world. That's the surprise. That's the mystery. That's one of the secrets of Christmas."

🌿 *Talk about it*

• Brother Gabriel keeps saying Christmas is a mystery. Do you agree with him? Talk about a time when Christmas seemed like a mystery to you.

• Read the story of the angel's appearance to Mary in the New Testament book of Luke, chapter 1:26-38. Then make a list of the advantages and disadvantages of agreeing to God's request.

• Name someone in your church, your family, or your neighborhood who is a quiet servant like Mary or the woman with the fruitcake. Talk about ways you might thank that person for the quiet things she or he does.

🌿 *Prayer*

Dear God,

We like being comfortable. We like having things our own way. But sometimes, just like you did with Mary, you call us away from what is comfortable and familiar and easy. You surprise us with chances to show kindness and service that are different—and sometimes scary or hard. In those times, help us look beyond our own needs to the needs of others. Give us courage and compassion so that your love might burst forth from us as well—in gifts and surprises as beautiful as a newborn child. Amen.

CHAPTER TWO

The Journey to Christmas

Christmas Eve is only two Sundays away, and the Junior Class of Woodland Street Community Chapel has a substitute for the holidays. His name is Brother Gabriel. He's new to the church. And in some ways, he is as mysterious as the amazing flannelboard he uses to teach the Christmas Story. It has already brought to life the angel's visit to Mary and the announcement that she will give birth to the Son of God. But class is far from over, and the children are eager to see more!

"Do it again!" begged Andy Chubb.

And we all joined in, "Yeah, do it again!"

Brother Gabriel put his hands in the air. "All right. All right," he nodded. "But you're going to have to quiet down a little bit. And you have to promise me one thing. This is a journey we're going on here, a journey that will take us all the way to Christmas. There will be more surprises, I can promise you that. But you know how surprises are. Sometimes they're good and, well . . . you've opened up enough Christmas presents to know what I mean."

"I do!" shouted Andy Chubb, waving his hand around until it looked like it would fly off the end of his arm. "Last year I thought I was gonna get this computer game. The package was the right size and everything. But when I opened it up, it was just a big box of underwear!"

"Boxers or briefs?" snickered Darrell Jackson.

"You don't have to answer that, Andy," grinned Brother Gabriel. "The important thing is that you know what I mean."

"Hey, Justin knows what you mean," chuckled my cousin Bill as he pointed at me. "He got a Malibu Barbie for Christmas last year!"

"Shut up!" I shouted. "It was the wrong name on the package, that's all. My dad just got mixed up."

"My mom says your dad is always getting mixed up," Bill muttered back.

"Quiet, now," said Brother Gabriel, more seriously this time. "What I want is for each of you to promise to stay on the journey until the end. Until Christmas comes. No matter how hard the journey gets. No matter what kind of surprises we find."

Then he looked around the room at each one of us.

"I promise!" said Andy Chubb, so excited he could hardly sit still.

"Me, too, I guess," shrugged Darrell Jackson.

Andrea looked very serious (which was difficult for someone who usually looked pretty serious in the first place!) "I promise too," she said.

"Yeah, sure," said my cousin Bill.

And then it was my turn.

"Justin?" Brother Gabriel asked. "How about you?"

I thought about it for a minute. "I just have one question," I said. "You told us this would be like a journey. Have you ever been on this journey before?"

Brother Gabriel smiled. "Many times," he answered. "And all I can tell you is that each time is different, and each time is the same."

"Surprises, right?" I said.

"Exactly!" he replied.

"All right, then," I said. "I promise too."

"Then let's have a look at the next picture!" he grinned.

Brother Gabriel shuffled through his old brown box and pulled out two more figures. Then he stuck them onto the flannelboard next to a couple of felt pillars.

"This part of the Christmas story," he explained, "took place both before and after the angel visited Mary. Watch. Listen. And see what happens."

Just like the first time, the figures started to change. One of them turned into a woman, an older woman. Not as old as my grandma, I thought, but older than my mom. The other figure turned into an old man, an old man who kissed the woman and then wandered over to where the pillars stood—pillars that grew into a whole building before our eyes.

"That's the temple! The temple in Jerusalem," Andrea said. "I saw a model of it once at the church we used to attend."

"Then who's the old guy, Brainiac?" asked Darrell Jackson.

Andrea looked annoyed. But all she did was shake her head and mutter, "I don't know."

"Watch," Brother Gabriel whispered. "Watch and you will see!"

The old man walked slowly past crowds of people who had gathered around the building, past the pillars, right to the center of the temple courtyard. Then he walked into a building and stood before an altar, where he set something on fire. Smoke rose from the altar, curling and climbing toward the ceiling. The old man watched the smoke for a minute, and then something caught his attention. A shadow? A sound? It was hard to tell. But when he turned his head to look, he was no longer alone. For there was an angel—the same angel who had appeared to Mary—standing at the altar's side.

The old man trembled and shook and clutched at his chest with one hand.

"Zechariah," the angel said, "please don't be afraid."

And that's when Darrell Jackson said, "Hey! I heard that!"

We all heard it. There were no cartoon bubbles this time. In fact, even the pictures looked more real.

"I haven't used this old board in a while," Brother Gabriel chuckled. "I guess it takes a while for it to warm up!"

Meanwhile, the angel was still talking.

"Zechariah," the angel continued, "like the smoke from this incense, your prayers have risen up to God himself. And he has sent me to give you his answer. Your wife, Elizabeth, will give birth to a son. And you are to call him John."

"John the Baptist!" Andrea burst out. "I *thought* I'd heard this story before!"

"But my wife is barren!" Zechariah protested. "She is well past child-bearing age. To raise her hopes now . . . I mean . . . how do I know what you're telling me is true?"

The angel spoke firmly. "All I can say is that I stand in the presence of God himself. And all I can tell you is that he has sent me here to deliver this good news. But because you do not believe me, you will remain silent—unable to speak a word—until what I have promised comes to pass."

And with that, the board froze.

"That wasn't very nice," said Andrea. "I mean, the old man already couldn't have children. And then the angel takes his voice away too."

"It was a punishment," said Darrell Jackson, "because he didn't believe what the angel said. That kind of stuff always happens in the Bible. I thought you'd know that!"

Andrea looked like she wanted to say something—something not very nice—when Brother Gabriel interrupted.

"Maybe it was something else," he suggested. "Maybe it had more to do with one of those Christmas surprises I've been talking about. Maybe it had to do with hope."

"Hope?" asked Andrea, suddenly angry. "Hope! What do you know about hope?"

"A great deal," said Brother Gabriel gently. "And I know a lot about prayer too. I know that women and men can pray and pray for something they really want, and still never believe that it might actually happen. Who knows how long Elizabeth and Zechariah prayed for a child? And who knows when they gave up hope? Gave up so much hope that even when the answer came, Zechariah would not believe it. And so his inability to speak became a sign, a sign of hope that an equally impossible thing—the birth of a son to an old and barren couple—might actually happen too.

"It's one of the surprises of Christmas, Andrea, that God offers not empty promises, but real hope." Then he turned to the board again. "Watch, and you will see."

The figures on the flannelboard began to move again. The old man walked out of the temple, unable to say a word. But the crowd that gathered for worship in the temple courtyard knew, just by looking at him, that something unusual had happened.

"He's seen a vision!" they whispered. And they pointed at his face and gasped.

The flannelboard focused on his face as well. It zoomed right up to him like one of those long-distance cameras. And that's when Andrea gasped too. For the old man's face had changed into the face of someone else.

"Who is it, Andrea?" asked Andy Chubb.

"It's my brother," Andrea answered, fighting back tears.

Andy tried to help, he really did. But in his typical Andy Chubb way, he said the totally wrong thing. "Does he want to have a baby too?"

Andrea shook her head as a smile forced its way through her tears (all right, so maybe it wasn't *totally* the wrong thing to say!).

Andrea's big brother is very troubled," said Brother Gabriel softly. "Isn't that right?"

Andrea nodded. "Things haven't been going very well for him lately. He lost his job, and his girlfriend dumped him, and he owes a lot of money. Everybody else in the family says he should just quit moaning and get up off his backside and find another job. But he seems—I don't know—too sad for that. He just sits at home all day, quiet—not happy like he used to be." And then Andrea whispered very quietly, "He told my mom that he doesn't want to live anymore."

"He needs a sign, Andrea," Brother Gabriel whispered back. "He needs a sign of hope, just like Zechariah did. Do you think you can be that sign, Andrea?"

Andrea shrugged her shoulders. "But how? What can *I* do?"

Brother Gabriel thought for a moment. "I'm not sure," he said. "Perhaps something small will do. A flower. A gift. A favor. Some sign that you care about him and value him. Or perhaps he just needs someone to listen—someone to put aside her homework or shut off the TV and try to understand what he's going through. I can't be sure what will work, Andrea, any more than the angel could be sure the old man would believe him. But I'm sure of this: if you pray for your brother, God will use you to be a sign of hope—just like he used that angel."

"I'll try," Andrea nodded.

Brother Gabriel smiled. But as he turned to the flannel-board again, someone knocked on the classroom door.

"Oh dear," Brother Gabriel muttered, "I knew he would be coming. I just didn't expect it so soon."

🌿 Talk about it

- Read about the angel's visit to Zechariah in Luke 1:5-25. How would you feel if an angel suddenly appeared to you? What would you do? What would you say?

- Brother Gabriel tells the children that Zechariah's inability to speak was a sign of hope—the angel's way of showing him that the promise would indeed come true. Can you think of any other "signs of hope" in the Bible?

- Is there someone you know who needs a sign of hope in his or her life—someone who has been through a hard time, like Andrea's brother? What could you or your family do this Christmas to help this person see that life can be better?

🌿 Prayer

Dear God,

Thank you for hearing our prayers. Thank you for answering them. And when the answers seem a long time coming, help us to be patient, help us to keep on believing. Help us to hope. Amen.

CHAPTER THREE

An Upside-Down World

❧

As the first class continues, the mystery of Brother Gabriel and his flannelboard grows deeper still. The board uses sound, not just pictures this time, to tell the story of the angel's visit to old Zechariah, the father of John the Baptist. And when the story is over, the board changes the old man's face into a more familiar one—the face of Andrea's sad and troubled brother. Brother Gabriel encourages her to be a "sign of hope" to her brother, just like the angel was to Zechariah. Can she do it? And more than that, how does Brother Gabriel know about her brother in the first place? And finally, who is the visitor—the visitor whom Brother Gabriel already expects—who is knocking on the classroom door?

Before Brother Gabriel could even say "Come in," the door flew open and my Great Uncle Harry stuck his head into the room.

"Just wanted to make sure everything was all right," he said sternly. "The women's class downstairs complained about shouting and strange noises [here he looked at Bill and me], and I know how rambunctious these boys can be."

"No. No, everything is just fine," Brother Gabriel assured him.

My great uncle glanced at Brother Gabriel, and I'm sure I saw something in that look that said he didn't like him, or trust him, or that he just couldn't figure him out. Then the look went away and he said, quite sternly again, "You have fifteen minutes left. We don't want the children to be late for the morning service." And then that look came back again, "You're new here, but it's still important that you understand these things." And finally he left, shutting the door behind him.

"I hate to say it," Darrell Jackson whispered, "but that man gives me the creeps!"

"Hey, that's my granddad you're talking about!" complained my cousin Bill. "And his great uncle!" he added, pointing at me.

To be honest, I didn't really want to get into that argument. Yeah, Bill and I were related, but it was like we were from two different families. His granddad (my Great Uncle Harry) was my grandmother's brother. And that's about where it ended. Their side was rich and successful. Our side wasn't. And it was the kind of thing that the one side never let the other side forget. We all went to the same church, of course ("It's a family thing," is all my mom would say), and because it was such a small church, we were always—I don't know—bumping into each other.

"Well, my grandma says he thinks he owns the place!" Darrell Jackson sniped back.

"He does not think that!" argued Bill. "People just say that because he works so hard. He's the Sunday school superintendent and the chairman of the church board . . ."

"And he plays a mean organ!" added Andy Chubb.

Bill and Darrell both glared at him.

"No, I mean it!" said Andy defensively. "I love that *oom-pa-pa* he puts in the middle of *A Mighty Fortress!*"

"We only have a few more minutes," Brother Gabriel

interrupted, "and there is one more part of the story I want to show you before you leave."

The figures on the flannelboard had turned back to felt. Brother Gabriel took away the pillars and the figure of Zechariah, but he left Zechariah's wife behind.

"Her name was Elizabeth," he explained, "and she was Mary's cousin. Six month's after Elizabeth discovered that she was expecting a child [here he smiled at Andrea] six months after God's promise came true, Mary came to visit her with news that she, too, would soon be giving birth to a son—Jesus, the Son of God!"

"So John the Baptist and Jesus were related," I said. "Sort of like Bill and me."

Brother Gabriel nodded and then placed the Mary figure next to Elizabeth. At once, they began to change. They grew and grew, bigger than any of the characters we had seen so far, until all we could see were the two faces, old Elizabeth and young Mary, looking at each other.

Mary greeted Elizabeth with a kiss. And as she did, Elizabeth's eyes opened wide in surprise and her mouth made the shape of an "Oooh!"

"When you greeted me just now," she said to Mary, "when you told me your news, my baby leaped inside me—leaped for joy! Don't you see? He knows already how special his little cousin will be. You and your baby are so blessed—and so am I—for God has granted me this visit with the very mother of my Lord!"

And then the picture changed. It was like the camera left Elizabeth and focused on Mary alone. Her face filled the flannelboard as she turned and looked at us, almost as if she was speaking directly to us!

"My soul magnifies the Lord, and my spirit rejoices in God my Savior, for he has looked with favor on the lowliness of his servant. Surely, from now on all generations will call me blessed; for the Mighty One has done great things for me, and holy is his name. His mercy is for those who fear him from generation to generation. He has shown strength with his arm; he has scattered the proud in the thoughts of their hearts. He has brought down the powerful from their thrones, and lifted up the lowly; he has filled the hungry with good things, and sent the rich away empty. He has helped his servant Israel, in remembrance of his mercy, according to the promise he made to our ancestors, to Abraham and to his descendants forever." (Luke 1:46-55 NRSV)

The words were really nice, but I wasn't sure I understood what they meant. I would have asked, but I didn't want to look stupid. Fortunately for us all, looking stupid was one thing Andy Chubb never seemed to care about.

"I don't get it!" he blurted out. "What's she saying, Brother Gabriel?"

"It's a kind of poem, Andy," Brother Gabriel explained. "It's Mary's way of celebrating the fact that she will be giving birth to God's own Son. But it's more than that. It's also a celebration of what Jesus will do when he comes—and his people after him. Watch. Watch and listen, and you will see."

We looked at the flannelboard, and there were both Mary and Elizabeth again, sitting side by side. But as we watched them, they changed—over and over again—like a chameleon's changing skin.

First they were covered with horrible red blotches.

Then they were painted with lipstick and makeup and stuff.

Next, they held babies, and men came and tried to tear the babies out of their arms.

After that, they were nurses, bent over a wounded soldier.

Then they were visitors at a place for the insane.

And finally they turned black, black as Darrell or Brother Gabriel, and sat there, side by side, in chains.

Brother Gabriel watched them with us, watched them sadly. And then he spoke. "Mary's poem announces that Jesus will turn the world upside down. That those who are used to getting the big presents—the rich, the powerful, and the proud—will get nothing. But those who have grown used to getting no gifts at all—the poor, the hungry, and the oppressed—will have more presents than they can count, so that every human life has dignity and meaning and value.

"That's why, when Jesus grew up, he went out of his way to touch the lepers that no one else would touch. And that's why he spent time with the outcasts of his society—the prostitutes and the tax collectors. And after he left this earth, his followers determined to do the same. They fought the evil of infanticide, for example."

"Infanticide?" asked Andrea.

"Baby killing," explained Brother Gabriel. "It was a common practice in Roman times if the father wasn't pleased with the kind of child he got. But that wasn't all Jesus' followers did to turn the world around. They started hospitals. They visited prisoners. And, at a time when most people visited insane asylums for amusement, they worked to make sure those poor souls were treated with kindness and care. And finally, some of them stood at the forefront of the movement to abolish slavery. . . ."

Darrell Jackson leaned back in his chair and looked at Brother Gabriel like he didn't quite believe him. "So how come there are still so many poor people and hungry people and oppressed people in the world today?"

Brother Gabriel sadly shook his head. "Evil, mostly," he explained. "As long as people are selfish and don't care about what happens to anyone but themselves, some folks are always going to get trampled on. But there's more to it than that. Turning the world upside down is a big job, and even though the followers of Jesus have been working at it for two thousand years or so, they know better than anyone that the job isn't going to get finished until Jesus himself returns. And finally . . ."

He was interrupted by a bang on the door and the gruff voice of Uncle Harry. "Church is about to get started. You should have been out of here five minutes ago!"

"And finally," Brother Gabriel concluded, glancing at the door, "as long as the followers of Jesus are mainly concerned with what goes on inside the four walls of their church buildings, they are never going to see Mary's poem come true or this wicked world turned upside down for good."

✿ *Talk about it*

- Read about Mary's visit to Elizabeth and Mary's poem in Luke 1:39-56. Go through Mary's poem and list all the good things God does for us.

- Talk about ways that God is using your church to do those kinds of things in your community. Or discuss ways that God might use your church in the future.

✿ *Prayer*

Dear God,

It's hard to imagine a world turned upside down. A world where the outcasts and the poor and the picked-on have their needs met before anyone else does. Maybe it's because that seems so impossible. Or maybe it's because we have grown used to seeing things as they are. So turn us upside down, we pray. Help us see the outcasts and the poor and the picked-on people as you see them. And then help us treat them as you would. Amen.

CHAPTER FOUR

Doing the Right Thing

One week has passed since Brother Gabriel introduced his amazing flannelboard to Woodland Street Chapel's Junior Class. The kids have never seen anything like it. And even though they can't begin to explain it, none of them is likely to sleep in this Sunday morning. Justin's Great Uncle Harry, however, seems to have his doubts—not because he's seen the flannelboard, but because Brother Gabriel is new to the church and not as particular about the rules as he is. Will the two of them get along? What part of the Christmas story will the children visit this week? And what surprises does the flannelboard have in store for them?

For the first time ever, I couldn't wait for Sunday school. Every day during the week, I thought about telling my mom what had happened. But whenever I worked up the courage or managed to come up with an explanation I thought she would understand, she was never available. She was getting ready for work or she was too tired after work or she was "dealing" with my dad. And let's face it, she probably wouldn't have believed me anyway. I had a hard time believing it myself. I kept wondering if the others had said anything to their parents; and when we got together again the following Sunday morning, I was kind of relieved to find out that everybody else had kept quiet too.

It's not that we were trying to hide anything. It's more like this: what happened to us was special. And I guess we wanted to keep it special, just among ourselves, so nobody would have the chance to spoil it.

We got to the room even before Brother Gabriel. Everybody was excited, talking and laughing and wondering what would be on the flannelboard next. But we quieted down quickly when we heard an even louder noise coming up the stairs. It was my Great Uncle Harry.

"And besides the noise," he shouted, "you kept those children a full five minutes past the last bell! I had parents calling me all week, wondering why their children were late for morning worship! 'Decently and in order'—that's how the Apostle Paul himself said that things should be done! And if I can't count on you to follow the rules—rules that have worked in this church for many years now—then I will have to find a substitute who can. Is that understood?"

We didn't hear Brother Gabriel's answer. In fact, when he walked into the room and slowly shut the door behind him, we tried to look like we hadn't heard the conversation at all.

Embarrassed—that was how I felt about what my great uncle had said. And everybody else looked pretty uncomfortable too—except for my cousin Bill, who had this nasty smirk on his face.

"All right, then," announced Brother Gabriel, clapping his hands together and smiling to save us from any more embarrassment, "let's get back to the Christmas story and see what surprises it has in store for us today!" Then he stopped, like he had remembered something, and looked at Andrea.

"How's your brother?" he asked.

"Pretty much the same," Andrea shrugged. "I tried to do what you told me. I made him some peanut butter brownies—they're his favorite—and I smile whenever I see him. And I prayed for him every day last week. But it doesn't seem to make any difference."

"Not yet, maybe," said Brother Gabriel, "but that doesn't mean it's not having some effect. Don't give up, Andrea. You're a sign of hope, remember?"

And then he tacked up his old flannelboard, just like he'd done the week before. And he pulled the Joseph figure out of the box and stuck it on the board, lying on top of a little felt bed.

"Quiet, now," Brother Gabriel whispered, "we don't want to wake him up. He's had trouble sleeping as it is."

"What do you mean?" shouted Darrell Jackson from the back. And just like he'd heard that shout, Joseph jumped and turned and tossed in his bed.

"Quiet!" Brother Gabriel repeated. "Be quiet and watch and listen."

Slowly we moved closer to the flannelboard. Slowly the board zoomed in closer to Joseph's face—so close we could hear him snore. Closer still, until we could feel each breath. And then everything went all fuzzy, and there were pictures and faces and voices jumping all over the place.

"What's happening?" whispered Andy Chubb.

"We're looking into Joseph's dream," Brother Gabriel explained softly. "It's the only way to understand his story."

First there was a party, with lots of singing and dancing. Mary and Joseph both looked very happy.

"It's their engagement," said Brother Gabriel.

Next, there were just the two of them. Mary had tears in

her eyes and she was pointing to her swollen belly.

"She's trying to explain, isn't she?" whispered Andrea. "About the angel and what he had to say."

But Joseph wasn't buying it. You could tell. He was angry at first, so angry he looked like he wanted to hit something—as angry as my dad looks sometimes when he's had too much to drink. But then he just turned and walked away. And that's when we could see the tears in Joseph's eyes.

"He loves her," Brother Gabriel said, "but he's hurt too. He just doesn't know what to do. He wants to believe her impossible story, but he can't. And so his hurt says, 'Expose her! Tell everyone what she's done!' And his love says, 'No. If you're going to call off the engagement, do it quietly to spare her the shame.' But there is another voice—another voice and another choice. Watch and see."

A tear fell from Joseph's face. But before it hit the ground, it grew wings and then burst into the shape of an angel.

"Joseph," the angel said, "don't be afraid to take Mary as your wife. As impossible as it seems, what she has told you is true. The baby she is carrying is God's own Son. And when he is born, you will call him Jesus, for just as the name means, he will save his people from their sins."

The dream started to fade then, and all of a sudden we were looking at the outside of Joseph's head again. There was his ear. There was his hair. But when we finally got a look at his face, it wasn't Joseph's face at all. It was the sleeping face of . . . Andy Chubb!

Everybody turned around at once. And there was Andy, looking more surprised than anyone.

"What am I doing on the flannelboard?" Andy asked Brother Gabriel.

Brother Gabriel shook his head. "It's a surprise all right," he chuckled. "We'll just have to watch and see."

Andy—the Andy on the flannelboard—woke up. He was wearing these pajamas with little cowboys all over them, and Darrell Jackson started to laugh.

"Shut up!" Andy shouted. "I don't even have any pajamas like that!"

"Yeah, right," my cousin Bill snickered. "The ones with the little teddy bears are in the wash!"

"No, I mean it!" Andy insisted. "Look! Look at the bed and the lamp and those old-fashioned pictures on the wall. That's not even my room!"

"Andy's right," agreed Andrea.

And everybody else went, "Oooooh!"

Andy went all red, but Andrea just sighed and rolled her eyes towards the ceiling. "I was hanging out with his big sister, okay? And we had to go into his room to get some paper or something."

"Or to leave a *luvvv* note," grinned my cousin Bill.

Andrea ignored him. "The point is that Andy is right. His room is a lot newer and a *whole* lot messier than the one on the flannelboard!"

"There," said Andy, missing the insult completely, "I told you so!"

Meanwhile, the Andy on the flannelboard was walking across the room. There was a bed on that side too. Andy shook whoever was in it, and a boy who looked a little younger rubbed his eyes and crawled out. Finally, they both went to a third bed, where they poked at the covers until a third boy— the biggest of them all—stood up to join them.

The three of them walked to the bedroom door and opened

it. There was a staircase in front of them, and they lined up—shortest at the front, tallest at the back—like they were going to march somewhere.

And that's when Andy gasped, "I don't believe it!"

"What? What!?" We all shouted.

"I know where this is!" he said. "I mean, I've never been there, but I've heard about it a million times. That's my grandma and grandpa's house—or it used to be. And the kid—the kid in the middle that looks like me—that's my dad!"

"No way!" said Darrell Jackson. "Your dad is the big guy downstairs with the beard and the bad jokes!"

"No, that's him, honest!" Andy insisted. "And I can prove it! In a minute, the three kids—my dad and his brothers—will walk down the stairs. And just as they reach the bottom, a big light will shine in their eyes."

Andy was right. Not a second later, the boys went down the stairs and were almost blinded at the bottom.

"It's my grandpa," Andy explained. "He had one of those old-time movie cameras, and my dad said that he needed really bright lights to make it work."

Andy was so excited now he could hardly stop, so we watched the pictures as he told us the story.

"They're going into the living room next," he explained. "See, there's the tree hanging on the wall."

"Hanging?" asked Andrea.

"Yeah," Andy smiled. "My grandpa cut the tree in half that year—right down the middle, lengthwise. He hung one half in the house and the other half on the front door, and he decorated them both! My dad tells us that story every year!

"Ooh, look! There's the train, the train my dad's granddad gave him. It was really old, and it would only run backwards! And my uncle is about to open his 'big present.' It's going to be something called a 'Time Machine.' You put these little plastic squares in it and they turn into dinosaurs."

"Cool!" said my cousin Bill. And everybody looked at him.

"Well, for little kids," he added.

The flannelboard was *our* "Time Machine," and we sat and watched and wondered at that Christmas day from long ago. Andy watched hardest of all, soaking in every little detail, and you could hear him moan when the picture started to fade.

"Please, Brother Gabriel," he begged, "can't we watch some more? My dad told me all about Christmas when he was a kid. But there's so much more I don't know anything about."

"You know about your uncles, don't you?" asked Brother Gabriel.

"Yeah. The oldest one was killed in Vietnam. And the younger one—well, Dad just said he got into a lot of trouble. He doesn't talk about him much. Come to think of it, he doesn't talk about anything from his childhood except Christmas."

Brother Gabriel spoke very quietly now. "That's because Christmas is the only time he really wants to remember. Your grandfather was a salesman, Andy, and he was away from home a lot. Your father grew up without him—without a father of his own really. Your grandfather's absence put a lot of pressure on your grandmother as well—pressure she handled by spending time away from home, time she might have spent with her children. So do you see what happened? Your father and his brothers had a nice house and nice things, but they never had much of a family."

"But *I* have a nice family!" Andy protested.

"Yes, you do," smiled Brother Gabriel. "And that's because of the middle boy in the picture there. The one that looks like you. Your one uncle left home as soon as possible, looking for another home in the army. But he died in the war a year later. And your other uncle went from trouble to trouble, hoping that someone—anyone—might pay him some attention. But your dad? Well, every family has one—a saver, the one who thinks he can hold everything together and make everything right. He did his best. He was only a kid, after all. But the only time things ever seemed right was at Christmastime. I can't explain why, and I don't think he can either. But for some reason, that unhappy family found joy together with the "Time Machine" and the train that ran backwards and that odd half of a Christmas tree. And your dad decided very early that no matter how bad his childhood was, his own children were going to have better ones."

The flannelboard changed again, and the face of Joseph appeared beside the face of Andy's dad.

"Do you see the similarity?" asked Brother Gabriel. "They both had it tough. They both could have taken the easy way out. But each of them decided to do the hard thing, the right thing, the surprising thing. They determined that good would come out of what looked so very, very bad."

Joseph was standing with Mary now, side by side on their wedding day. Andy's dad was all grown up, sitting on the sofa with Andy and his sisters. And both of them—Joseph and Andy's dad—were smiling.

"It's the same smile, see?" said Brother Gabriel. "The smile that Joseph is wearing. The smile on your father's face. And the smile on the face of that little boy in the cowboy pajamas. The surprising smile. The optimistic smile. The smile that believes, against all hope, that someday everything will be better. That someday, every day will be just like Christmas."

 ## *Talk about it*

- Both Joseph and Andy's dad faced hard situations in their lives. What was it that made them want to overcome those situations instead of giving up or doing something bad in return?

- What was the hardest thing you ever had to do? Were you able to overcome it in a good way? How did you do that?

- Is there someone in your life like Andy's dad—someone who had to do something hard and good so that your life could be better?

Prayer

Dear God,

Sometimes life gets really hard. People hurt us or disappoint us or turn their backs on us when we need them. And sometimes, sadly, those people are the ones we love the most in the entire world. When that happens, dear God, help us not to be overwhelmed by our pain or anger or bitterness. Bring us through those hard times. Help us to forgive. And fill our hearts with the love that looks beyond the hurt to something better, something brighter. Amen.

CHAPTER FIVE

Into the Flannelboard

Story by story, the flannelboard seems to be getting more and more real. The children have just looked into Joseph's dream and also into the history of Andy Chubb's family, and they have come face to face with the kind of love and patience that overcomes hardship and pain. But class is not yet over. And, as amazing as their journey has been so far, they have yet to discover the full wonder of Brother Gabriel and his flannelboard.

The flannelboard faded. Brother Gabriel plucked off the felt figures of Mary and Joseph and then reached into his box again.

"Time for a geography lesson," he announced.

"Geography!" moaned my cousin Bill. "I hate geography!"

"Me too!" joined in Andy Chubb. "All those squares and circles and triangles!"

"That's geometry, Chubb-face!" sighed Darrell Jackson. "Geography is about places like Paris, Rome, London . . ."

"And Palestine," interrupted Brother Gabriel, sticking a long, thin strip of cloth on the board.

"What did I tell you?" shouted Andy Chubb. "That's a rectangle. Or maybe it's a parallelogram. I always get those two mixed up."

"It's Palestine," repeated Brother Gabriel, "the country where Jesus was born." Then he drew two lines across the shape.

"Palestine was divided into three parts," he explained. "Galilee was in the north. Samaria was in the middle. And Judea was at the bottom. Now, Joseph and Mary lived in Nazareth, a little town in Galilee, at the top here."

"But I thought Jesus was born in Bethlehem," said Darrell Jackson.

"That's right," nodded Brother Gabriel. And he pointed to a spot way down on the bottom piece.

"I don't get it," Darrell continued. "Why did they go all the way down there to have a baby?"

"That's another one of those Christmas surprises," grinned Brother Gabriel. "And not a very nice one, now that I think about it. You see, the Roman Empire controlled the country of Palestine at the time—along with much of the rest of the world. And it just so happened that the Roman emperor, Caesar Augustus, decided to conduct a census."

"Census?" asked Andy Chubb.

"He wanted to count everybody," Andrea whispered.

"Math again!" sighed Andy.

"Anyway," Brother Gabriel went on, "in order to count the people more easily, everyone had to go back to his hometown. And because Joseph's family originally came from Bethlehem, that is where he had to go."

"But it looks like such a long way!" said Andrea.

"Seventy miles or so," nodded Brother Gabriel. And then he gave us this funny kind of look. "So are you ready for the journey?"

As soon as he said that, the flannelboard started to change. The long, thin piece of cloth turned into a real country, and it was almost like we were in an airplane, flying over it. There was a lot of brown, with a thin blue line running down one side. Slowly, the ground got closer, and everything got bigger and bigger. We could see hills now, and towns and trees; and the blue line turned out to be a river. The picture on the flannelboard shifted here and there, like it was looking for something. And then we saw it—clouds of dust, rising from a wide, flat road. And walking along the road, a long line of travelers.

"I told you this journey would be full of surprises," said Brother Gabriel. "What I want to know is—are you ready for the biggest surprise of them all?"

We looked at each other and nodded. I didn't know what anybody else was thinking, but I couldn't imagine surprises any better than what the flannelboard had shown us already. As it turns out, I didn't have much of an imagination.

"All right then, Bill," Brother Gabriel announced, "you get to go first. Just take a deep breath, and it will all be over in a second."

"Go?" asked Bill. "Go whe . . ."

Before he could even finish his sentence, there was a "bang!" and a "whoosh!" and my cousin Bill was sucked straight into the flannelboard! And I don't mean that he crashed into it or smacked into it. I mean he disappeared into it. He was gone!

I jumped up. But before I could do anything, Andrea disappeared too. And then—I don't know how it happened really—one minute I was in the classroom, and the next minute I was coughing up dust and dodging a donkey's tail!

"Over here!" called a voice. "Come over here!"

It sounded like Andrea but, because of the dust, I couldn't see her anywhere.

"Andrea!" I shouted. "Is that you?"

The donkey's tail flew past my face, and it occurred to me that it had to belong to the biggest donkey in the world!

"Quick!" the voice called again. "Get out of the way or you're going to get smashed!"

I followed the voice this time, but I still couldn't see Andrea. There was just the donkey and the dust and this enormous black fly buzzing around in front of me. And then the fly turned around and hollered.

"Would you hurry up!" it shouted.

What could I do? I didn't want to get smacked by that enormous tail, so I followed the fly—and eventually we landed on the donkey's back.

Landed? Landed! Safe at last, I looked at my hands. I looked at my feet. And I realized that I was a fly too!

"Andrea?" I asked, staring at the other fly.

"Justin?" she asked back. And I nodded my big bulgy-eyed head.

"We're inside the flannelboard, aren't we?" she said.

"I think so," I answered. "And I bet we're on that road we saw—the one that leads to Bethlehem."

"I don't think I like this," Andrea groaned. "Brother Gabriel wouldn't let us get hurt, would he?"

"I don't think so," I said. "But he did warn us that there would be surprises—even some we wouldn't like. I guess this is one of them."

"But flies! Why flies?"

I buzzed up and down a few times, trying out my wings. "My guess is that we're supposed to watch and listen. Isn't that what Brother Gabriel is always saying? And what better way to do that than as flies? I mean, nobody pays attention to them."

"Except people with fly swatters," she moaned.

"Yeah, well, I don't think they had fly swatters in Biblical times," I said. "So all we have to do is keep clear of that donkey's tail and everything should be fine. Let's have a look around."

I flapped my wings and took off. It was kind of fun. Andrea followed me. We flew along the donkey's back until we ran into the bright blue robes of the person riding the donkey. We flew up behind the person. It was a long way! And then we buzzed around to have a look at the person's face.

We should have guessed, really. It was Mary. She was tired and sweaty. She kept her eyes closed most of the time and rocked back and forth to the motion of the donkey below her. But every now and then, the donkey would stumble a little or lose its footing, and she would grunt and grimace like it really hurt.

"Look," whispered Andrea, flying down near Mary's belly. "She could have the baby any time now. I wonder how far we are from Bethlehem."

"I don't know," I shrugged. "All I can see out there is dust. Maybe we should ask the donkey."

"The donkey?" asked Andrea.

"Sure. We can talk. Maybe the donkey can talk too." And then I remembered what happened just before Andrea and I got sucked into the flannelboard. My cousin Bill had disappeared, which meant that he was in here somewhere too. Maybe it was a hunch. Maybe it was just wishful thinking. But I smiled a little fly smile. "As a matter of fact," I added, "I'll bet you anything the donkey can talk! Come on!"

We buzzed down to the donkey's head, between his flicking ears, past his blinking eyes, and hovered right in front of his nose.

"Bill," I buzzed. "Bill! Is that you?"

The donkey just snorted and sighed. "Yeah, it's me all right."

"Well, we're here too. Me and Andrea!"

But Bill didn't seem too happy to see us. "My feet are killing me!" he moaned. "My back is gonna break any minute now. And my allergies are acting up again." Then he let out a sneeze that nearly blew us into the back of the camel up the road.

"A donkey! Brother Gabriel turned me into a donkey! Just wait till I tell my grandpa on him!"

"But Bill," I said, "don't you know who's on your back?"

"I don't care," Bill grunted. "I just want out of here. I want to go back to class and sit down and have a nice glass of something cold to drink."

And then he stopped and folded his front legs and rested his head on the ground so suddenly that Mary shifted and groaned and cried out.

"Bill! Bill!" buzzed Andrea. "You have to get up. You have to keep going. It's Mary on your back! She can't have her baby here in the middle of the road!"

"But I don't want to. I don't want to!" Bill hee-hawed.

I didn't know what to do. Bill had always been a crybaby. Everybody in the family knew that. If he got a splinter or stubbed his toe or something, he usually screamed so hard you thought his leg had been cut off! On the other hand, it couldn't be easy to be a donkey. And not one of those Christmas-pageant donkeys either. This was the real thing. And it looked like hard work to me. So I guess I felt sorry for him. And maybe that's why I said what I said.

"I'll tell you what, Bill. If you keep going, if you get Mary to the stable, then . . . then . . . then I'll clean your room for a month or let you copy my math homework or anything. Please!"

Mary was moaning real loud now. And Joseph had started to shout and wave his staff around.

"Really?" whispered Bill.

"Really," I buzzed. "Just so you get her there!"

So Bill got up. And without another complaint, he carried Mary all the way to Bethlehem.

It took a long time to find a place to stay. The town was packed! But in the end, one very kind innkeeper pointed us to a stable at the back of his house. It wasn't much: just a hole in the side of a hill, with some hay and a manger and one or two sleepy animals. But Joseph and Mary acted like it was a mansion! He helped her off Bill's back and made her a bed in the straw. Andrea and I just buzzed around my cousin's donkey ears.

"Good work, Bill," said Andrea.

"Yeah, you did good," I agreed.

But Bill just sat there and stared sadly at Joseph and Mary. "No, I didn't," he snorted at last. "I was grumpy and selfish, and

I almost ruined the whole Christmas story." Then he did something I had never, ever seen him do before. He said, "I'm sorry. I was just tired and hot, that's all. But when you think about it, it *was* kind of special, wasn't it? Being the one who carried Mary to Bethlehem. I guess that's pretty good, huh?"

"Better than being a fly," I buzzed.

And then Bill started to yawn—a big, toothy donkey yawn. So I said goodnight and flew off with Andrea towards the ceiling. We settled on the edge of a little hole in the wall.

"Brother Gabriel was right about all the surprises," she said. "We've had a day full of them!"

"I'll say," I agreed. "And maybe the biggest surprise was finding out that my cousin isn't such a donkey after all."

"I guess that counts," she buzzed. "Well, if we're not going back to class, we'd better get some sleep too." And she flapped her wings to lift off.

"Hey," she said, "I can't seem to fly. There's something sticky on the ledge."

"Here, let me try," I said. But my feet were stuck too. And then I heard something creeping through the hole behind us. Something hairy and black with a mouthful of teeth.

"I think we've got one more surprise to come," I shuddered. "Remember those bad surprises Brother Gabriel warned us about? I think there's one behind us now!"

 *Talk about it*

- Did you ever have the chance to do something good for someone else but, because it looked hard, you didn't really *want* to do it? Talk about that time. And if you did manage to do it, what made you go through with it? And how did you feel afterwards?

- If you could be anybody in the Christmas story, whom would you want to be and why? Who would you definitely not want to be?

- There are many legends about the animals in the stable and the gifts they brought to the Christ child. What other animals might have been in the stable that night? Talk about what gifts they might have brought to the Christ child—gifts unique to the abilities and characteristics God gave them. And then think about yourself—the unique and special person that God made you to be. What kind of gift might you give to the Christ child?

Prayer

Dear God,

We have all been donkeys from time to time. You have asked us to do something good for someone else. But we have been stubborn— moaning about our own needs and not being concerned about the needs of others. Forgive our noisy braying. Forgive our stiff backs, our selfishness, and our pride. Help us to be good donkeys, bearing one another's burdens and trusting you to help us carry the weight. Amen.

CHAPTER SIX

The Mystery of the Manger

Andrea, Justin, and Bill have been sucked into the flannelboard—and into the Christmas story as well! Andrea and Justin are "flies on the wall," watching the story unfold. Bill is the donkey—the donkey that carried Mary to Bethlehem. And even though he's not thrilled with his long ears and tail, he manages, in the end, to make the best of it. He's resting now. And Andrea and Justin would like to do the same. But a nasty surprise, in the shape of a hungry spider, is creeping up on them. Where are Andy and Darrell and Brother Gabriel? And the time—what about the time? They've been away for a day at least. How will they ever explain where they have been?

The spider slowly crept up behind us. I flapped my wings until they hurt, but I couldn't move. My feet were stuck fast to the ledge. I wanted to shut my eyes, I really did. But flies don't have eyelids, so that was no help either. In the end, I decided to do what I always do at school whenever Josh Adams, the class bully, starts beating on me. I looked straight into the spider's eyes and started to scream!

"You're nothing but a big, old, hairy arachnid! That's what you are! And you can eat us if you want, but we won't taste any good! We'll make you sick, that's what we'll do. And, besides, we're not really flies anyway. We're kids. And if we ever get out of this, you can bet that you're gonna get stomped!"

I figured the spider might just understand. I figured he'd probably eat us anyway. But I never figured on what actually happened.

"Chill!" the spider said. "It's Darrell! I've been looking for you guys everywhere. Is that Bill beside you?"

"No, it's Andrea," Andrea grunted. "Bill's the donkey."

"Works for me," chuckled Darrell.

"How about Andy?" I asked. "Did he come too?"

"The cow," Darrell sighed. "The big red one in the corner."

"Hi, Andy!" Andrea called. "How do you like being a cow?"

"Just fine," Andy mooed. "Although I think I would rather be a pangolin. I've always liked pangolins. And marmots. They're nice too. But a cow is all right, I guess. How do you like being a fly?"

"It was great," Andrea said, "until we thought Darrell was going to have us for lunch!"

"Darrell wouldn't have eaten you," Andy said. "Would you, Darrell?"

"No way!" Darrell grinned. "I was already full. You see, there were these maggots down in the hay . . . . Gee, I hope they weren't anybody we know!"

"Stop it!" cried Andrea. "We're all here, and you know it. Well, except for Bother Gabriel."

"I'm here too!" called a voice from the sky as a dove flew

into the stable and landed on the edge of the manger.

"So who's back in the room?" I asked.

"Nobody," Brother Gabriel cooed. "I locked the door, just to be safe."

My cousin Bill looked up at me with his donkey eyes. "Grandpa's not gong to like that," he said.

"We'll be back in no time," Brother Gabriel assured us. "Everything will be fine. In the meantime, we have the chance to witness the biggest Christmas surprise of them all!"

Darrell unstuck us and we all made our way down to the manger to join Brother Gabriel. Andrea and I flew, and Darrell swung down on a long, webby string. But just as we got there, Mary groaned and cried out, and Joseph knelt down beside her.

"The child is on its way," he assured her. "It won't be long."

"I don't think I want to watch this," groaned Darrell Jackson.

"Me neither," mooed Andy Chubb. "We saw this movie in health class once . . ."

"We'll let them have their privacy, of course," Brother Gabriel said. "But it's nothing to be embarrassed about. Each and every one of you came into the world in exactly the same way—kicking and screaming and gasping for breath. In a word—helpless."

"What's the surprise then?" asked Darrell.

Brother Gabriel spoke very slowly. "The surprise is that the helpless baby who is being born right now is also the one who made the world and everything in it!"

"But how is that possible?" I asked.

"He alone knows," Brother Gabriel smiled. "The surprise,

however, is not *how* it happened, but *why* it happened."

"So God could understand us," Andrea said, "that's why he became just like us." And then her eyes lit up. "That's why you turned us into spiders and flies and donkeys . . ."

"And cows!" added Andy Chubb.

"So we could understand how it works," finished Andrea.

Brother Gabriel gently shook his head. "No, Andrea," he said, "not quite. You see, God has always understood us. He made us, after all. He knows us better than we know ourselves. No, the reason he became one of us was so that *we* would be convinced, once and for all, that he really understood. It was for *our* understanding, not for his."

Mary cried out again, harder than she had before. And then we heard a baby cry.

"God, naked and small. God, wailing and wet. God, gasping for breath and hungry for his mother's milk—so that we might never doubt his understanding of our lives or his concern for what we face. That is the surprise. That is the great mystery of Christmas!"

"But why in a stable?" asked Andy. "Why not someplace more comfortable and warm?"

"So that no one would be left out," Brother Gabriel explained. "So that the poorest of the poor—those who, like this couple, have no place to call their own—would be confident of God's understanding and care as well."

And so we stood and watched—the animals in the stable—as Joseph cleaned the baby and wrapped the baby and laid him in his mother's arms. It was normal and natural—like any family. But it was amazing too.

Then we heard a bang. And then another. A knock-knock-knocking that would not go away.

"Oh dear," said Brother Gabriel. "Perhaps it was a mistake to lock that door after all. I think we'd better be going!"

Brother Gabriel blinked his dove eyes and, in an instant, we were back in our seats. We were kids again. And there wasn't a feather, an antenna, or a donkey's tail among us. But Uncle Harry's voice had joined the knocking now.

"Open the door this minute!" he shouted.

"I'm sorry," Brother Gabriel apologized as he undid the latch and let my uncle in. "We were in the middle of something important, and I didn't want us to be disturbed."

"That's no excuse!" shouted Uncle Harry, getting louder by the second. "How dare you lock me out of my own Sunday school room? What if there had been an emergency? And the time! Have you looked at the time?"

Brother Gabriel glanced at the clock on the church wall. "We have a minute to spare," he said. And we all looked at each other, surprised.

"But we were away for hours!" whispered Andrea.

I nodded my head. "I know!"

"Well, you *would* have been late, wouldn't you," my Uncle Harry ranted on, "if I hadn't come up here and banged on this door? And look at these children. They're a mess! Shirts not tucked in. Faces dirty. And that hefty boy over there—his hair looks like it hasn't been combed for weeks!"

Andy Chubb licked his palm and patted his hair down. "It's a cowlick, sir!" he giggled.

"This is no time for nonsense!" Uncle Harry shouted. "I'm

very serious." Then he turned again to Brother Gabriel. " I had reservations about you from the start. But Mrs. Jones, the lady in charge of finding substitutes, assured me you would be suitable. 'We can't find anyone else at this short notice,' she told me. 'It's just for a few weeks,' she insisted. But I was right, wasn't I? You don't just take someone off the street, someone who has only been coming to our church a little while, someone unaware of our traditions, and put him in charge of our children! Someone we hardly know. Someone we can't trust. Someone, who's, well . . ."

"Black?" asked Darrell Jackson. "Is that what you were going to say? It's because he's black, isn't it?" Darrell was shouting now. "It's just been me and my Grandma up until now. But I hear what people say. And she does too. 'You have to watch those neighborhood kids.' 'Better lock up the money.' 'There's a dollar missing from the offering, and we all know who took it!'

"But then Brother Gabriel started coming, and I thought maybe things would be different. But, no. Now you want to get rid of him too! Well, you can keep your stupid church and your stupid rules and your stupid, sit-still-and-sing-your-songs-like-you're-some-kind-of-robot services! I'm leaving, and I'm never coming back!"

And with that, Darrell pushed his way past Uncle Harry and Brother Gabriel and ran out of the room.

"Darrell, wait!" called Brother Gabriel.

"Come back here this minute, young man!" shouted Uncle Harry. "There's no running in this church!"

But Darrell was already gone.

• Find one of your baby pictures. Take a good look at it. What do babies do all day? And what do others have to do for them? Make a list, and then talk about what it must have been like for the God who made the whole universe to have to experience those things too.

• List five good things that people get to experience in their lives. List five bad things that sometimes happen. Then talk about how it might help to know that God had to face those things too.

🌿 *Prayer*

Dear God,
  Thank you for coming close to us.
  Thank you for being born like us.
  Thank you for crawling and crying and reaching out for your mother's milk.
  Thank you for showing us
  that each and every one of us
  is valued and special and precious in your sight.
  Amen.

CHAPTER SEVEN

Shepherds and Angels

❦

It's Christmas Eve morning. And the Woodland Street Chapel Junior Class is a mess! Uncle Harry, the Sunday school superintendent, has threatened to get rid of Brother Gabriel. Darrell Jackson has said he will never come back to the church again. And the flannelboard's journey through the Christmas story still has a long way to go. Will the class ever get the chance to finish the journey? Or is it over for good, even before Christmas has really begun?

The week before Christmas Eve didn't feel much like Christmas to me. My mom was busy with her job and the shopping and all the Christmas preparations. She just kept getting more and more tense. And my dad? Well, my dad somehow managed to get invited to every Christmas party in his office building, so he staggered home every night, drunk. It was a bad combination—my mom's tension and my dad's drinking. So I spent a lot of time in my room—thinking.

Would we ever see Darrell again? He was really angry when he left.

Would Uncle Harry let Brother Gabriel be our teacher anymore? And if he did, where would the flannelboard take us next?

And would my cousin Bill call me and hold me to my promise to clean up his room?

As it turned out, I didn't have to worry. When Darrell's grandma heard what happened, she took him by the ear and made him apologize to Uncle Harry and Brother Gabriel and to every lady in the women's class downstairs. It didn't seem fair in a way, but she was a big lady, and if she had hold of my ear, I would have done whatever she said too!

As for Uncle Harry—well, he might not have liked what Darrell said (and maybe it wasn't even true; I don't know), but I can say for sure that he wouldn't want anybody to *think* he was prejudiced. So, according to my mom, anyway—who heard it from one of the deacon's wives—he told Brother Gabriel he could teach for one more week. And that would be it.

As a matter of fact, everything seemed pretty normal (or as normal as a class with that flannelboard could be) when we showed up on Sunday morning. Darrell was quieter than usual (and he kept rubbing his ear!). Brother Gabriel seemed a little calmer too. I was just thinking that maybe everything would be all right when my cousin Bill bent over and started to whisper in my ear.

"Yeah, yeah," I interrupted. "I'm still going to clean your stupid room. You don't have to remind me."

Bill looked surprised. "Thanks!" he said. "I forgot all about that. No, what I was *going* to say is that Grandpa is going to sit in on our class this morning. I tried to talk him out of it, but I think he wonders what we're doing in here, with the locked doors and strange noises and everything. First he has to talk with the preacher about the candlelight service, but then he's coming up."

"Does Brother Gabriel know?" I whispered back.

"Yes, Brother Gabriel knows," said Brother Gabriel (demonstrating remarkable hearing for a man of his age, I thought). "And Brother Gabriel intends to do things just as he always does. I never asked you to keep this a secret. I only asked you to stay with me till the journey's end. And if someone else wants to join us on this journey, then that's all right with me."

For the third time—for the *last* time, I figured—Brother Gabriel tacked the flannel sheet to the edge of the blackboard. Then he opened up that old brown box, took out a pile of figures, and arranged them on the board.

There were triangular shepherds with pipe-cleaner staffs, cotton-ball sheep, and a sky full of white felt angels with golden glitter glued to their wings.

There were no surprises this time, I thought. Everyone knew which part of the Christmas story we were watching.

And then a breeze blew—right out of the flannelboard! A sharp, nighttime breeze. And suddenly we were shepherds too—sitting on the hill behind other shepherds. The room was gone. Completely gone! And a shivering little lamb tried to snuggle under my arm.

Andy Chubb started to say something, but Brother Gabriel held up his hand and whispered, "Be quiet. Just watch. Watch and listen."

The angels began to sing. And I guess I was expecting—I don't know— "Hark the Herald Angels Sing" or "O Come, All Ye Faithful" or "Joy to the World." But that's not what came out of their mouths at all.

The song was beautiful, but also different from anything I

had ever heard. It went around and around in loops, the same words over and over again. There was no beginning and no end. There were lots of different voices too. Low voices and high voices and middle voices—but no harmony. They all sang the same thing:

"Glory to our God on high
Peace to earth where men abide!"

The song grew louder and louder. Louder than thunder. Louder than fireworks on the Fourth of July. Louder than anything I had ever heard. It bounced off the hills and the stars. It sank into the ground and filled up the sky. And just when I was sure that Uncle Harry and the women's class and everyone in church would come crashing into the room to tell us to be quiet, the music stopped.

All but one of the original shepherds disappeared. And the angels moved solemnly across the sky and settled into neat rows, like windows in tall buildings down in the valley below our church. Rivers formed, washing right up near the buildings—first one, then two, then three.

Suddenly we were back in our regular clothes again, and we all knew exactly where we were.

"It's downtown!" shouted Andrea. "From the top of Mount Washington. We went there on a field trip once."

"The city looks great!" I said.

"Yeah," Andy Chubb agreed. "Look at all those lights!"

"I wonder who that shepherd is?" asked my cousin Bill.

And then the shepherd turned around, suddenly a shepherd no more.

It was my dad.

"Wh-what's he doing there?" I asked. I was feeling a little nervous. A little scared.

"Probably looking for an open liquor store," snickered Bill.

Brother Gabriel put his hand on my shoulder and talked to me like I was the only one in the room.

"He's waiting. He's watching. That's what he's doing. Like the shepherds that night. And I think he's just about ready to hear the angels sing."

"But he doesn't come to church or anything," I said. "He hates it. He thinks it's stupid. He even makes fun of my mom and me sometimes. And besides, he doesn't even believe in God!"

"Lots of people don't," Brother Gabriel answered. "But often the god they don't believe in isn't the God who's really there, anyway. It's a god they heard about on TV or had a bad experience with at some church somewhere. But deep inside, they're still watching and waiting. Waiting for someone to point them to Bethlehem and show them the way to the God of love, the God who came in the manger. They need an angel to guide them there. And tonight, my young friend, that angel is you."

"Me? But what am I supposed to do? I'm just a kid."

"You can lead him to the stable," Brother Gabriel said softly. "That's what you can do. There's a Christmas Eve service tonight, isn't there? Ask him to come."

"But he never comes! My mom asks him every year."

"Yeah, well, *my* mom says it's because he can't find his way out the front door," sneered my cousin Bill.

"Shut up, Bill!" I shouted, and I turned around to punch him.

"Calm down!" Brother Gabriel ordered. "And Bill," he added, "I want you to keep quiet until we're finished here."

Then he turned to me again. "Justin, " he said, "don't wait for your mom to do it. Invite him yourself when you get home. Then wait and see. He's been on the hill. His experiences and yearnings and his questions have brought him there. And, yes, his drinking did too. It's peace he's looking for. Peace from the criticisms of your mother's family. Peace for his troubled soul. The peace the angels sang about. Up until now he's tried to find it in the bottom of a bottle. But you can take him to the stable, to the place where it's really found. The door of his heart is open. And God wants to be born in him tonight."

I shrugged my shoulders. I looked up at Brother Gabriel. "I'll try," I said. "I'll try."

And as soon as I'd said it, we were back in the room again.

❧ *Talk about it*

• The song the angels sang promised that the baby born in the stable would bring peace. What do you think peace is? Is there more than one kind of peace? And how does Jesus bring us peace?

• Do you know anyone like Justin's dad, someone who is looking for peace but can't seem to find it? What might you be able to do this Christmas to lead that person to the one who can bring them peace?

• Is there someone you are not at peace with? What could you do this Christmas to make peace between yourself and that person?

❧ *Prayer*

Dear God,

The angels' song said that Jesus would bring peace. But when we look around the world, we still see so much conflict. Conflict between nations and races and ages. And conflict inside us, as well, as we struggle to find peace in our lives. Lead us to the stable, we pray. And help us lead others too. Show us the peace you have for us there—the promise of the man in that sleepy child. The peace of his words, the peace of his deeds, the peace of his cross. Amen.

CHAPTER EIGHT

Star-Watchers' Dreams

The journey is back on track again. The flannelboard has taken the children to see the shepherds, and Justin has seen his father as well—waiting to hear the angels' songs. He has promised to invite his father to the candlelight Christmas Eve service. But before that can happen, class has to finish. And there is one more part—one very important part—of the Christmas story left to tell.

My cousin Bill got up out of his seat and went to the door. "I wonder what's keeping Grandpa," he said. "Maybe I should go and look for him."

"You'll miss the next part of the journey," said Brother Gabriel. And then he got this really strange look in his eyes and added, "I'm sure he'll join us when he needs to."

Then Brother Gabriel took the shepherds off the flannelboard and stuck three fancy figures in their place.

"It's the Wise Men!" shouted Andy Chubb. "I wondered when they were gonna show up."

"I thought they were kings," said my cousin Bill. "*We Three Kings*—you know, like the song."

Brother Gabriel stuck a huge felt star on the top right corner of the flannelboard.

"It's more likely that they were star-watchers," he explained.

"Men who believed they could figure out what God was doing by looking carefully at the world God had made—particularly the stars."

"But they didn't believe in *our* God, did they?" asked Andrea. "At my other church we learned that they came from Babylon or somewhere, and that they worshiped idols."

"They came from the east," Brother Gabriel said, "that's all the Bible tells us. And, yes, it's likely that they worshiped some other kind of god. But the beauty of this story—its surprise—is that God used their curiosity about gods in general to lead them to the true God. Watch and listen, and you'll see."

The wise men—or star-watchers—walked across the bottom of the flannelboard as if they were in a parade. One. Two. Three. And then a fourth star-watcher appeared out of nowhere. And a fifth. And a sixth!

"Wait a minute!" said my cousin Bill. "There are only supposed to be *three* kings, right?"

"We don't know," smiled Brother Gabriel. "The Bible says there were three different gifts—gold, frankincense, and myrrh. And people have always assumed that they came from three different men. But who can say for sure?"

"And what about the camels?" asked Andy Chubb. "There must have been camels. Hey, I can be a camel if you want! I was a pretty good cow."

"That won't be necessary, Andy," said Brother Gabriel. "But we can put in some camels, if you want."

"And a pangolin?" Andy added.

"There weren't any pangolins in the Bible, Chubb-face,"

grunted Darrell. It was the first time he had said anything all morning.

"But there weren't any Eskimos, either," Andy answered, "and there's one on the flannelboard."

He was right! Behind the six wise men and their camels came a team of huskies and an Eskimo sled.

"Look! There are Indians too!" Andy shouted.

"Native Americans," Andrea corrected him without even looking at the board.

"No, Indians! From India!" he insisted. "With turbans and sandals and stuff. Oh, look. The Native Americans are right behind them."

A world full of people had joined the parade now. Chinese, Japanese, African, Maori   all marching after that star.

"But that wasn't how it was," I said to Brother Gabriel.

"How it was? How it is? How it might be?" Brother Gabriel grinned. "Who can tell what the flannelboard is up to? All we can do is watch and see."

The night breeze blew our way again, an even colder breeze this time. And suddenly we were at the back of that line.

"I wonder where we're going?" asked Andy Chubb.

"To Bethlehem, Chubb-face," groaned Darrell Jackson. "Where do you think?"

"Maybe not," said Andrea. "We could be going to Herod's palace."

"That's right!" said Andy, happy to be defended for a change. But then he went and blew it. "So who's Herod?" he asked.

"Herod was the Jewish king at the time," Brother Gabriel explained. "He had to answer to the Romans, of course, but he was in charge of the country of Palestine—and he defended his throne ruthlessly.

"When the star-gazers told him they were looking for the newborn king of the Jews, Herod was both furious and fearful," Brother Gabriel continued. "So he sent the star-gazers to find out exactly where the child was living. He told them that he wanted to honor this new king as well. But he really intended to murder the child."

"What a mean guy," said my cousin Bill.

"Some people will do anything to hold on to their power," Brother Gabriel sighed. "Herod killed his wife, an aunt, an uncle, and even two of his sons because he believed they were trying to take his throne from him."

"Well I hope we're not going *there!*" said Andy Chubb.

"It's easy enough to find out," said Brother Gabriel. And he tapped the person ahead of us on the shoulder. The man was one of those South American Indians you see sometimes on the *National Geographic* specials, with paint on his face and feathers hanging from his ears.

Brother Gabriel talked to him. We couldn't understand what they were saying, but when Brother Gabriel turned to us again, he had a relieved smile on his face.

"Nothing to worry about," he said. "They've already been to visit Herod, and now we're on our way to see the Christ child."

"So we're going back to the stable?" I asked.

"I don't think so," Brother Gabriel answered. "The star-gazers came some time after Jesus was born—maybe as much as two years. So we'll probably be going to a house."

"But how will we all fit in?" asked Andrea. "There must be

hundreds of people in this line!"

"Watch and see," grinned Brother Gabriel. "I don't think I have to tell you that you just might be surprised!"

We arrived at the house at last. It was an ordinary looking place, like all the others on the street. Nothing fancy. And not very big, either. But that didn't keep us from getting in. Person by person, the line moved into the house. And just when I thought the walls would burst open, the line kept moving. It was like one of those clown cars you see at the circus, and we were the clowns!

The house kept filling up until finally it was our turn to walk through the front door. And that's when the surprise came—when we realized that we weren't walking into a house at all.

"It's our church!" gasped Andy Chubb. "Look! There's the pulpit and the stained glass windows and the pew my family always sits in that's wobbly at one end!"

Andy was right. It was our church. Mary and Joseph and little Jesus were sitting down by the communion table. Every seat was filled, every eye was focused to the front, and every lip was moving with some kind of prayer or praise. And in that way, it seemed to me, it wasn't much like our church at all.

"Darrell," Brother Gabriel called, "come here a minute. I want to ask you something."

Darrell pushed past the rest of us, and Brother Gabriel laid a hand on his shoulder.

"Tell me what you see," he whispered.

"People," Darrell shrugged. "Lots of people. More people than ever come to *our* church."

"Tell me about the people," Brother Gabriel continued.

"They're all different," Darrell answered.

"Different how?"

"Different clothes. Different languages."

"Different colors?"

"Yeah, okay. Different colors. So what? This isn't our church. This just *looks* like our church. It's made up. It's pretend."

"Like a dream?" asked Brother Gabriel.

"Yeah, okay." Darrell shrugged again.

"Then why not make it *your* dream?" Brother Gabriel said.

"Because it'll never happen," Darrell muttered.

"Not if you leave," said Brother Gabriel. "Not if your grandma leaves. The dream will never come true then." And here he turned to the rest of us. "And that's a shame. Because what you see before you here is God's dream for your church too."

"God's dream?" asked Darrell.

"Of course," smiled Brother Gabriel. "Think of the neighborhood your church is in. Once upon a time, only white people went there, mainly ordinary folk who worked down at the mill. But in the last twenty years all that has changed. As those white families died or moved out to the suburbs, black families and brown families and yellow families and mixed families moved in to take their places. But the families in the church, except for Darrell and his grandma—and now me—are all white. And I, for one, find it hard to believe that the God who sent a star to announce the birth of his Son to other lands and other races can be very happy with that."

"But what can we do?" asked Darrell.

"You can stay," said Brother Gabriel. "You can dream—dream of the day when the inside of your church really looks like this. And you can be stars, each of you, reaching out to your friends at school or in the neighborhood and inviting them along—regardless of their accents or the color of their faces. It might take some time. And if your parents and grandparents are resistant to the idea, your church might not look like this until you are grownups yourselves. But you can continue to dream until the dream comes true. Watch. Watch and listen."

A door opened down at the front of the church. It was the door the minister usually came out of just before the service began. But the man who walked out of that door wasn't our minister at all. He was young, maybe in his thirties. And he was black.

"Hey, Darrell," said Andy Chubb, "that guy looks like he could be your older brother."

"But I don't have an older brother," said Darrell.

And that's when the minister spoke. "I'd like to welcome all of you to our service today. My name is Pastor Darrell Jackson. I grew up in this church, and I can't tell you how pleased I am to see you all here."

"What was. What is. What might be," whispered Brother Gabriel. "God's dreams come true against all odds. That is the wonder. That is the surprise. That is the great mystery of Christmas!"

🌿 *Talk about it*

• Take a look around your church next Sunday. How many different colors of faces do you see? Is there a mix of black and white and yellow and brown? Or is there mainly one color (or only one color)? Why do you think that is? And what could you or your church do to change that?

• Brother Gabriel told the children that God had a dream for the Woodland Street Church. He said that God had a dream for Darrell too. Do you think God has a dream for your church? And for you? Has God ever given you hints about what that dream might be? Talk about that dream.

🌿 *Prayer*

Dear God,

    Too often we see the world in black and white.
    Those who are like us and those who aren't.
    Good and bad, in and out, them and us.
    But you sent your star to the ends of the earth to gather all people at the feet of your Son. Thank you for that star. Thank you for that dream. Make that dream come true for us, as well—in our homes, in our communities, in our churches.
    Rescue us from black and white.
    And help us dream in color—
    All the colors of the world! Amen.

CHAPTER NINE

Into the Future

Mary and Joseph. The shepherds. The Wise Men. The journey to Christmas should be over. But there is still a little class time left. And the flannelboard doesn't look like it's ready to finish. So what's left to see? Maybe it has something to do with Uncle Harry and his promised visit, and the one Christmas character the children have not yet met. Maybe it has to do with the biggest surprise of all!

I just thought of something," whispered Andy Chubb. "If we're down here, then who's up in our classroom?" And he ran out of the sanctuary and up the tower steps.

"Wait!" I shouted. "We're in the future . . . or in the flannel-board . . . or something." And I turned to Brother Gabriel. "Aren't we?"

"Why don't we find out?" he said calmly. So we followed Andy up the stairs. He got there first, but I was right behind him. And when he threw open the door, who was there waiting for us but Uncle Harry!

"Where have you been?" he demanded to know. "I've been waiting here for five minutes!"

"On a little . . . field trip," grinned Brother Gabriel as he walked into the room. "Have a seat, please. Our lesson is almost over."

"I'll stand, thank you," grunted Uncle Harry. "Never can tell when I'll be needed downstairs." Then he pointed at the flannelboard. "Haven't seen one of those in years," he said. "It's all videos now, they tell me."

We looked at the flannelboard too. We all looked. And there were the three felt wise men, just as we had first seen them!

"But this is a rather special flannelboard," said Brother Gabriel. "And I don't think that anyone here would disagree. It's full of surprises. Just like Christmas." And then he smiled at the rest of us. "Isn't that right?"

"Yes," I nodded.

"Absolutely!" Andrea agreed.

And Andy Chubb just giggled and mooed!

Brother Gabriel peeled the wise men and the star off the board. In their place he stuck up three shiny gold figures with pipe cleaners at their sides and round silver things in front of them.

"Soldiers," he explained, "Herod's soldiers."

Somebody—Andy, I think—said, "Boo!"

But Uncle Harry just grunted again. "I can't say I think much of your artwork," he said. "We had much better figures when I was a boy. At least you could tell what they were!"

"You'll be able to tell who the next figure is all right," said Brother Gabriel. "Every story needs a villain. And this story has one of the most wicked villains of them all!" Brother Gabriel shuffled through his box. "We've talked about him already, haven't we, class?" Then he got this worried look on his face and shuffled some more. Finally he sighed and lifted up his head.

"I apologize," he sighed. "I'm afraid I've misplaced the figure of Herod."

"Preparation," muttered Uncle Harry. "The bedrock of good teaching!"

But Brother Gabriel ignored him. "It must have dropped out of the box on the way up here," he said. "I don't suppose . . ."

Before he could finish his sentence, however, the flannelboard started to change, just like it always did. Palace walls grew up around the soldiers. Marble floors spread under their feet. And even Uncle Harry managed to look amazed.

"Remarkable!" he gasped. "How do you do it?"

"It's a surprise," I said.

"A mystery," added Brother Gabriel.

And Uncle Harry just stood there and shook his head. "Amazing. Show me more!" Then he stared, open-mouthed, as we all watched things begin to happen in the flannelboard.

The soldiers bowed to someone off the picture. I was pretty sure who it was.

"We're sorry, your majesty," one of them apologized. "The star-gazers are gone. There is no sign of them anywhere."

A voice—a voice from off the picture—cursed. "Then we must make other plans."

It was Herod. It had to be Herod. We shivered just to hear him speak.

"Go to Bethlehem," the voice ordered, "go back and find every male child that is two years old and younger. Find those children and kill them all. The newborn king is bound to be among them."

"But, Your Majesty," objected one of the soldiers, "the children have done nothing!"

Suddenly a knife flashed as it shot from off the board straight into the soldier's heart.

"There will be no 'buts,'" the voice continued. "Do your duty. Do it now!"

The soldiers left, dragging their dead comrade behind them. And everything went quiet.

"Is that it?" asked Uncle Harry. "I want to see more. Show me more!"

"We need the Herod figure," I explained.

"Maybe you should look again," said Darrell to Brother Gabriel.

"There's no need," answered Brother Gabriel, sadly shaking his head. "You see, Herod has been in the room all along."

As soon as he said that, Uncle Harry got sucked straight into the flannelboard!

"He's not gonna like that," moaned my cousin Bill.

"Maybe not," said Brother Gabriel, "but he asked to see more. He wanted to go on the journey. And this is the part he needs to travel."

"What's the meaning of this?" cried Uncle Harry from inside the flannelboard.

"It's like he can see us!" I said.

He *can* see us," answered Brother Gabriel, "just as well as we can see him."

Uncle Harry ranted on. "How dare you dress me up like Herod!" he growled. "We've had our differences, I know. But this is uncalled for!"

If I were Uncle Harry, I would have been shocked or surprised or afraid. But he was too angry, I guess, to care about being in the flannelboard.

"Watch and listen," Brother Gabriel told him, "and you will see why you are wearing Herod's clothes."

The picture changed. Uncle Harry was still dressed like Herod, but Herod's palace had turned into our classroom. The whooshing sound returned, and suddenly we were in the classroom too. Or at least it looked like our classroom.

"It's all dusty," moaned Andy Chubb.

"And look at those cobwebs!" said Darrell. "They're huge!"

"And kind of spooky too," added Andrea. "What happened, Brother Gabriel?"

"You'll have to ask Herod," Brother Gabriel said.

"What? Huh?" asked Uncle Harry, dazed now from all the jumping around. And, thankfully, a lot calmer too. "I don't know what you mean."

"We're in the church classroom—*your* church classroom— twenty years in the future," Brother Gabriel explained. "It's empty, as you can see. And so is the church itself. Vacant. Unused. Abandoned. And the children want to know what happened."

"Well, how am *I* supposed to know?" grumbled Uncle Harry. "In twenty years time, I'll probably be dead!"

"Probably," nodded Brother Gabriel. "But it's my guess that your ghost will still be rattling around this place. So I'll ask you again: how did this happen?"

Uncle Harry shrugged. "You seem to have all the answers. Why don't you tell us?"

"It's Herod, don't you see?" Brother Gabriel sighed. "It's all because of Herod."

"Herod?" I asked. "I don't get it."

Brother Gabriel opened the classroom door and led us all down the cracked and creaking stairs. And as he walked, he explained.

"Herod wanted control, complete control. It was power that lay at the heart of his villainy. And when that power was threatened, he was willing to do anything so he would not lose it. If that meant sacrificing the innocent children of Bethlehem, so be it. It was a price that Herod was willing to pay."

We were standing in the sanctuary now, and it was even more rundown than our classroom had been. Some of the pews were gone. The fancy overhead lights were smashed and so were lots of the stained glass windows. It was really sad.

Uncle Harry was quiet now, as he looked around at his church—or at what would *be* his church. And even though he kept wiping them away, you could tell there were tears in his eyes.

We all felt a lot like crying ourselves as we stared at our church.

"But why am I dressed up like Herod?" Uncle Harry asked at last. "Are you blaming me for all this? I've given my life to this church."

Brother Gabriel gently put his hand on Uncle Harry's shoulder. "I know you have," he whispered. "But the sad truth—the truth you know in your heart—is that you think, somehow, that you now own this church. That it's yours to control. But if you continue on that path, you will discover what Herod discovered—you will have to sacrifice the children."

"Sacrifice the children?" asked Uncle Harry.

"Well, look around you. They're gone, aren't they?" said Brother Gabriel. "Gone to other churches, hopefully. Or maybe gone from the faith completely. But gone from this place certainly, because there was no room here for their laughter, their hopes, and their dreams."

"The dream!" shouted Darrell suddenly. "What about the dream, Brother Gabriel? The church we saw before. You said *that* would be our future."

"It could be," Brother Gabriel nodded. "Why don't you tell Harry all about it, and see what he thinks."

"Well, there were lots and lots of people," Darrell began. And as soon as he spoke, we could hear muffled voices out in the hall.

"And they were different kinds of people," Andrea continued, "black people and Asians and Native Americans . . ." And as she named each group, they suddenly appeared, sitting around us and moving through the pews— pews that were clean and shiny now!

"Oh, and Darrell was the minister!" added Andy Chubb. "Only he was a grown-up Darrell—not Darrell like he is here."

"And people were singing and praying just like Jesus himself was here," I said. And with that, the dream was real again— like it was when we'd followed the wise men into the house.

"I've never seen the place so full!" Uncle Harry marveled. "Or so happy, either." Now the tears that rolled down his wrinkled face seemed to come from a different place inside his heart. And he didn't try to wipe them away.

"It's your choice," said Brother Gabriel. "The nightmare or the dream."

"There's no choice at all!" Uncle Harry said. "I want the dream. I want *this* church. And I'll do whatever I have to do."

"Then you'll have to accept some things," Brother Gabriel smiled. "New leaders. New ideas. And an openness and welcome to every new and different face God sends your way. That's what it will take. It won't be easy—especially for you."

"I'm willing to try," Uncle Harry said, "really I am." Then he looked around at each one of us. And he smiled. I don't remember him ever smiling at us like that. "I don't want to lose the church," he said. "And I don't want to lose these children. I'm willing to do it for them."

Brother Gabriel again put his hand on Uncle Harry's shoulder. "Then everything should be all right." As soon as he said it, we returned to our classroom, and Uncle Harry was no longer dressed like Herod (but he no longer looked like the old Uncle Harry either!).

And then the flannelboard flicked on for one last time. Mary was riding on a donkey again, but this time she had her little boy on her lap. Joseph was walking at their side.

"The angel we saw in the dream said we should escape into Egypt," she explained to little Jesus.

"See?" said Brother Gabriel to Uncle Harry. "The dream is coming true. The child is safe. And I think that now your children are safe too."

• Why do you think Brother Gabriel gave Uncle Harry Herod's clothes to wear? Was Uncle Harry really as bad as Herod? And did Uncle Harry have any good characteristics? If so, what were they?

• What is it about a church that attracts people? And what do you think drives them away? Make a list for each category. How does the church you attend stack up to those lists? What could you and your family do to make things better?

• What is the church for anyway? What is its job?

🍃 *Prayer*

Dear God,

  We like to get our own way. But sometimes getting our own way means that others don't get what they need. That was Herod's problem. And some awful things happened as a result. So help us, we pray, when we're too bossy, too controlling, or too concerned about what we want. And show us the bigger picture, like you showed Uncle Harry. Help us see the good that can come from giving up what we want and letting others have their way. Amen.

CHAPTER TEN

The Secret of Christmas

❧

The time has arrived for the Christmas Eve service. And there are still a lot of unanswered questions. Will Andrea's brother start feeling any better? Did Justin ask his dad to the service? Will his dad come? And what will it mean for everyone now that Uncle Harry has seen the flannelboard too?

The Christmas Eve candlelight service always started at 7:30. And, unlike most of our church's services (where no one would even begin arriving until 7:29), people came early to this one. Maybe it was the decorations. Maybe it was all those pine and candle-smoke smells. Or maybe they just wanted to be sure the service ended on time so they could go home and open their presents. All I know is that I was there early for that service—in fact the whole class was—because Uncle Harry had called around that afternoon and asked us to arrive early.

I had never seen Uncle Harry so happy or so excited about anything. He looked like Scrooge on Christmas morning. And I wouldn't have been surprised at all if he had slipped me a shilling and asked me to buy the biggest turkey in town!

"I want you to tell everyone what happened with the flannel-board, with Brother Gabriel!" he explained our class. "Well, not *everything.* They'd never believe you. But tell them what you learned about the Christmas story—about Christmas."

Then he turned to Brother Gabriel. "That's all right with you, isn't it?"

Brother Gabriel smiled. "That was the whole point," he said. "The surprises—the secrets—of Christmas are for real, as real today as they were when they first happened. I think that's something *everyone* should know."

"You mean we have to give a speech?" asked Andy Chubb nervously.

"Not a speech," said Uncle Harry. "Just tell them what you learned."

"I learned how to moo!" Andy answered. "Do you want me to tell them that?"

"Why not?" said Brother Gabriel. "And you might want to mention what you learned about Joseph too."

"Oh yeah," Andy grinned. "You know, my dad told us those stories again today—about when he was a kid—and they were better than ever!"

"I could talk about signs of hope," Andrea beamed. And then it was like she just couldn't hold it in any longer. "My brother got a job!" she shouted. "And he's coming to the service tonight!"

Brother Gabriel grinned and gave her a hug. I wanted to congratulate her too. But I just couldn't—I guess because I was afraid someone might bring up the job I had been given to do. Oh, I'd asked my dad. But he acted just like he did every year. He grunted and he shrugged and he said it was just for kids.

"Is everybody ready?" asked Uncle Harry at last. "Does everybody have some idea of what they are going to say?"

We looked at Brother Gabriel, and we looked at each other, and we nodded. Brother Gabriel gave us a smile that said everything would be okay.

The church looked more beautiful than it ever had before. The candle flames shone fuzzy and warm against the stained glass windows. Pine branches and holly branches hung from every sill. Even the big plastic Mary and Joseph with the light bulbs inside looked nice, as they huddled with the plastic shepherds at the foot of the communion table.

The carols sounded better too. Maybe it was because Uncle Harry was playing the organ with more energy than he had in years. Or maybe it was because I was noticing the words—for the first time, I think—and the story they tried to tell. It was like some of those carol writers had been in the story too. And as I glanced at Brother Gabriel, I couldn't help wondering how old that flannelboard really was.

When the songs had finished, our minister announced that we would be doing something special this year—that some of us had been part of a very special Sunday school class and that he had noticed a big change (here he looked at Uncle Harry!) because of it. And that's when we went forward, one by one, to talk about what we had learned.

Andrea went first. She did a really good job. She told the story of the angel's visit to Zechariah and the sign of hope he was given. And then she said that we should all try to be signs of hope to each other—helping each other and building each other up—because we never knew if somebody around us might be about to give up hope.

Andy went next. Somewhere in the middle of telling how

great it was to be a cow and get milked and have people feed you chunks of hay (oh, and how much *better* it might be if you could go into a story where there was a pangolin), he managed to say a thing or two about how God wanted us to do our best, even if things were hard for us.

My cousin Bill didn't have a lot to say. He just told everybody how great he thought it was that God would leave a comfortable place like heaven to come and live in our world, where things weren't nearly so nice. He figured that God must love us a lot to do that for us.

Darrell, on the other hand, talked for ages. I think he was taking that "you're-gonna-be-a-preacher-someday" thing way too seriously! Or maybe it was because half his family had shown up—brothers and sisters and cousins and a whole pew full of aunts in huge flowery hats! They "Amen-ed" him and "Hallelujah-ed" him (and I think I even saw Uncle Harry join in a time or two!) when he talked about how Jesus had come to show God's love to *all* people, and to bring all people together in the power of that love.

And then it was my turn. To be honest, I didn't know what I was going to say. I got up out of my pew and walked to the front, but when I turned around to face the congregation, I froze. Not because I still hadn't figured out what to say but because, way at the back of the church, there stood my dad!

It would have looked stupid to cry. But that's what I wanted to do. So I blurted out, as fast and as loud as I could, the only thing I could remember. It was the words—the words from the song the angels sang: "Glory to our God on high! Peace to earth where men abide!" And then I said it again, because I still didn't want to burst out bawling.

And that's when somebody out in the crowd realized that there was a certain rhythm to those two lines. (Or maybe they guessed I was about to burst into tears.) So they started clapping and chanting it along with me. And soon the whole church was shouting it—not so pretty as the angels had sung it, maybe, but pretty powerful all the same.

And I could tell (because I looked!) that my eyes weren't the only ones wet with tears. And that's when Uncle Harry hit the organ, hard and loud like he had never played it before. He played "Hark the Herald Angels Sing," and that's how the service ended. Well, except for all the hugging and handshaking afterwards.

My dad came downstairs for punch and cookies, and even though he didn't say much, it was enough.

"Good job up there," he whispered to me. "That's how I like my sermons—short and to the point." Then he went off to find my mom, who had run into the choir room with a handful of hankies for about the fifth time!

I turned around, and there was Andy standing behind me, his mouth crammed full of cookies.

"Bruffer Gabriel wants to fee us," he mumbled, crumbs spilling out everywhere. And he pointed upstairs to our classroom. When Andy and I got up there, Brother Gabriel was already talking.

"I've just been telling the others," he explained. "I got a call from work this afternoon. There's an emergency in one of our other . . . offices. It looks like I'm being transferred."

"So you won't be coming to our church anymore?" asked Andrea.

"I'm afraid not," Brother Gabriel sighed, "and I'll miss that. I'll miss all of you very much."

"But what about the dream?" said Darrell. "I thought you were gonna be here for that."

"It's *your* dream now," Brother Gabriel grinned as he looked at all of us. "And judging by that crowd Darrell brought with him tonight, it's a lot closer to coming true than even I might have hoped for!"

"Does Grandpa know?" asked my cousin Bill.

"He does," Brother Gabriel nodded. "And he knows what he needs to do to keep the dream—to keep *Christmas*—alive here. But I'm counting on you kids to remind him from time to time, in case he forgets!"

"We'll never forget," said Andy Chubb, wiping the chocolate from around his mouth. "You were the best teacher we ever had." Then he ran over to Brother Gabriel and hugged him. And one by one, the rest of us hugged him good-bye too.

Parents started calling for us then, and I guess my dad still hadn't found my mom, because I was there with Brother Gabriel after everyone else left. I watched as he packed up the old brown box. But before he closed it, he reached in and handed me one of the figures.

It was the angel.

"Glory to our God on high!" he smiled. "And peace to earth where men abide. That's the mystery. That's the surprise. That's the great secret of Christmas: when we respond to God's love—and love each other in turn. No wonder that's the song the angels chose to sing."

"Angels," I repeated. I looked at him really hard then, and I felt goosebumps. "You mean angels like—like—*Gabriel?*"

The old man smiled at me again and walked me to the door.

"It's like I told you," he said. "You can't trust Christmas. It sneaks up on you when you least expect it!"

Then he closed the door behind me. And even though I waited no more than a second or two, when I opened it again and peeked inside, Brother Gabriel was gone.

Talk about it

- If you had to give a speech on what you learned about Christmas from reading the story of Brother Gabriel, what would you say?

- Each of the characters in the story was changed by meeting Brother Gabriel—some a little, others a lot. Have you ever been changed by something that happened at church or at a camp or at a retreat? Talk about what happened to you there.

Prayer

They were all looking for a king
To slay their foes and lift them high.
Thou cam'st a little baby thing
That made a woman cry.

O Son of Man, to right my lot,
Naught but Thy presence can avail.
but on the road Thy wheels are not,
Nor on the sea Thy sail.

My fancied ways, why should'st Thou heed?
Thou com'st down Thine own secret stair.
Com'st down to answer all my needs.
Yea, every bygone prayer.

(from the poem "That Holy Thing" by George MacDonald)